This Book Belongs To:

Kevin

THE RAND McNALLY BOOK OF
Favorite Nursery Classics

Illustrated by ANNE SELLERS LEAF

RAND McNALLY & COMPANY

Chicago

Established 1856

CONTENTS

adapted by Dorothy Bell Briggs

JACK
and
the Beanstalk

ONCE there was a poor widow who had an only son, named Jack. He was good-natured and affectionate but lazy. As time went on, the widow grew poorer and poorer until she had nothing left but her cow. And all the time, Jack grew lazier and lazier.

One day Jack's mother said to him, "To-morrow you must take the cow to market. The more money you get for her the better, for we have nothing left to live on."

Next morning Jack got up earlier than usual, hung a horn around his shoulder, and started out with the cow. On the way to market he met a queer little old man.

"Good morning, my lad," said the queer little old man. "Where may you be going with that fine cow?"

"I'm taking her to market," replied Jack.

"As if you had wit enough to sell cows! A bit of a lad that doesn't even know how many beans make five!"

"Two in each hand and one in your mouth," answered Jack, with a quickness that would have made his mother proud.

"Oho!" laughed the queer little old man. "Oho! Since you know beans, suppose you look at these," and he held out his hand, filled with rainbow-colored beans. "I'll give you all these for your cow."

"That would be a good bargain," thought Jack. So he traded the cow for the beans and hurried home.

"Look, Mother," he said gleefully, as he poured the beans into her lap. "I got all these pretty beans for the cow."

"You stupid boy!" she cried. "Now we shall have to starve." And she flung the beans out of the open window.

The next morning Jack woke early. He ran into the garden and found a beanstalk had sprung up during the night from the beans his mother had thrown away, and had grown so quickly its top was out of sight.

Jack began to climb, and he climbed and he climbed until he reached the top. He stepped off into the sky and walked on until he met a beautiful woman with a face like a star.

Now the lady was a fairy and she knew what Jack was thinking and answered him without his asking any questions.

She told Jack he was in a country that belonged to a wicked Giant. This Giant had killed Jack's father and stolen all his gold and precious things. Jack had been only a baby at that time, and his mother had been too sad ever to talk to him about it.

"If you and your mother are ever going to be happy again," said the fairy, "you must punish that Giant." She whispered in Jack's ear, telling him what to do. Then she left and Jack walked on.

Toward evening he came to the door of a castle. He blew his horn, and a cook as broad as she was tall opened the door. "I am very tired and hungry," said Jack politely. "Can you give me supper and a night's lodging?"

"You little know, my poor lad, what you ask," she sighed. "A Giant lives here and he eats people. He would be sure to find you and eat you for supper. It would never do!" And she shut the door.

But Jack was too tired to go another step, so he blew his horn again, and when the cook

came to the door he begged her to let him in. She began to cry, but at last led Jack into the kitchen. Soon he was enjoying a good meal and quite forgetting to be afraid. But before he had finished there came a *thump, thump, thump* of heavy feet, and in less than no time the cook had popped Jack into the great oven to hide.

The Giant walked in sniffing the air. "Fe Fi Fo Fum! I smell the blood of an Englishman! Be he live or be he dead, I'll grind up his bones to make my bread!" he thundered.

"You are dreaming," laughed the cook, "but there is something better than dreams in this dish." So the Giant stopped sniffing and sat down to supper.

Through a hole in the oven Jack peeped out and watched the Giant eat. When all the dishes

were empty, the Giant bade the cook, "Bring me my hen."

She brought a much-ruffled hen and put it on the table. "Lay," shouted the Giant, and the hen laid a golden egg.

Again and again the Giant shouted his orders in a voice of thunder, and again and again the hen obeyed, till there were twelve golden eggs on the table. Then the Giant went to sleep and snored so loud that the house shook.

When the biggest snore of all had shaken
Jack out of the oven, he seized the hen and ran
off as fast as he could to the top of the beanstalk.
He climbed quickly down and carried the wonderful hen to his mother. Day after day the hen
laid its golden eggs, and by selling them Jack
and his mother might have lived in luxury all
their lives.

But Jack kept thinking about that wicked Giant who had killed his father, and of the fairy's command. So one day he climbed the beanstalk again. This time he had dressed himself to look like a different person, as he did not want the cook to know him. And, sure enough, when the woman came to the door, she did not recognize the lad she had hidden in the oven.

"Please," said Jack, "can you give me food and a place to rest? I am hungry and tired."

"You can't come in here," answered the cook. "Once before I took in a tired and hungry young runaway, and he stole my master's precious hen that lays golden eggs."

But Jack talked to the cook so pleasantly that she thought it would be unkind to grudge him a meal. After Jack had a good supper, the

cook turned over an empty kettle and hid him under it. And it was none too soon, either, for in stalked the Giant, *thump, thump, thump* sniffing the air. "Fe Fi Fo Fum! I smell the blood of an Englishman! Be he live or be he dead, I'll grind up his bones to make my bread!" he bellowed.

"Stuff and nonsense," laughed the cook. And she placed his supper on the table.

After supper the Giant shouted, "Fetch me my harp." And the cook brought in a beautiful harp with strings of pure gold.

"Play!" commanded the Giant, and the harp began to play all by itself. Soon the Giant's snores drowned the sweet music. Then Jack jumped from under the kettle and seized the harp. But no sooner had he slung it over his shoulder than it cried out, "Master, Master!" For it was a fairy harp.

Jack was frightened and ran for his life toward the top of the beanstalk. He could hear the Giant running behind him, *thump, thump, thump.* Jack reached the top of the beanstalk and slid down it as quick as lightning, calling out as he went, "Mother, Mother! The ax, the ax!"

Jack's mother, holding out the ax, met him as he touched the ground. There was no time to lose, for the Giant was already halfway down. With one slashing blow Jack cut the beanstalk. There was a crash, and the Giant lay at his feet in the garden. Then Jack told his mother all the story. And as for the wonderful beanstalk it never grew again.

Little
RED RIDING-HOOD

ONCE UPON A TIME there was a little
village girl who was as sweet as sugar and
as good as bread. Her mother loved her very
much, and her grandmother was even fonder

of her. This kind grandmother had made her a pretty red cloak with a hood, in which the child looked so bright and gay that everyone called her Little Red Riding-Hood.

One day her mother made some cakes and
said to her, "Go, my child, and see how your
grandmother is. I hear she has been ill. Take
her one of these cakes and this little pot of
butter."

So Little Red Riding-Hood set out at once to see her grandmother, who lived in another village.

As she walked through the woods she met a big wolf. He would have gobbled her up

then and there, but some woodcutters were
near by and he did not dare. But he did ask
her where she was going. The little girl did
not know it was dangerous to talk to a wolf,
and so she said,

"I am going to my grandmother, to take her this cake and little pot of butter."

"Does she live far off?" asked the wolf.

"Oh, yes," answered Little Red Riding-Hood. "She lives beyond the mill you see way down there, at the first house in the village."

"All right," said the wolf. "I'll go and visit her too. I will take this way, and you take that way, and we'll see who gets there first."

Soon the wolf arrived at the grandmother's cottage and knocked at the door—tap! tap! "Who is there?"

"It is your own Little Red Riding-Hood," said the wolf, making his voice sound as much like Little Red Riding-Hood's as he could.

The good old woman, who wasn't feeling
well and so was in bed, called out, "Pull the
string, my dear, and the latch will fly up."

The wolf pulled the string and the door opened. He sprang upon the poor old grandmother and swallowed her all in one gulp, for it was more than three days since he had had a bite. He did not feel very well after that, but he shut the door, put on the grandmother's cap, and stretched himself out in the old woman's bed to wait for Little Red Riding-Hood.

By and by Little Red Riding-Hood came knocking at the cottage door—tap! tap! "Who is there?"

At first Little Red Riding-Hood was frightened at the hoarse voice of the wolf. But she made up her mind that her grandmother must have a cold.

"It is your own Little Red Riding-Hood," she answered. "I have brought you a cake and a little pot of butter which Mother has made and sent you."

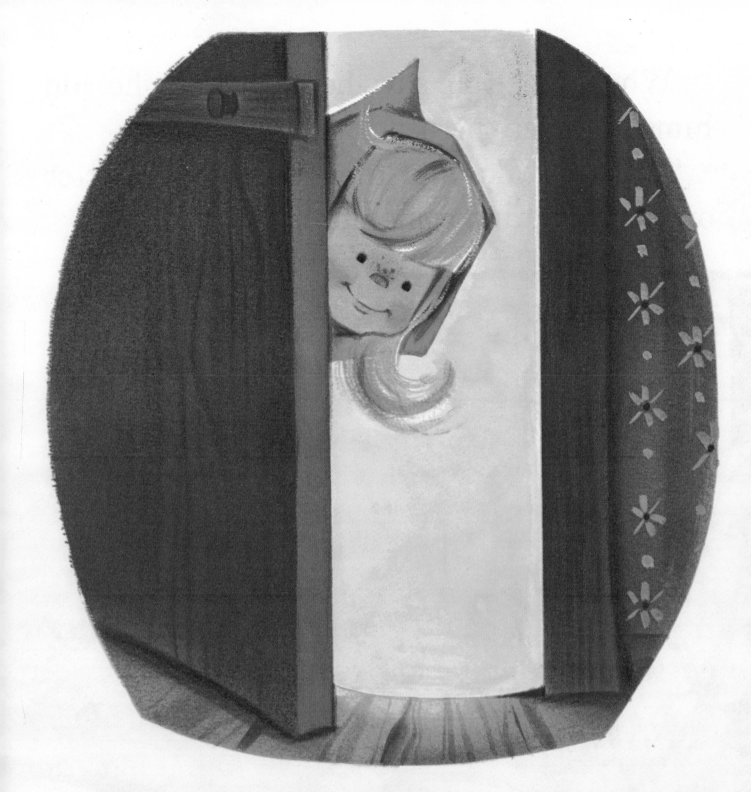

Then the wolf called out, softening his voice as well as he could, "Pull the string, my dear, and the latch will fly up."

Little Red Riding-Hood pulled the string and the door opened.

When the wolf saw her come in, he hid himself under the bedclothes and said,
   "Put the cake and the little pot of butter on the shelf, and come here."

And so Little Red Riding-Hood put the cake and butter on the shelf and went over to the wolf. She was very much surprised to see how strange her grandmother looked in her night clothes and said,

"Grandmother, what great arms you have!"
"The better to hug you, my child!"
"Grandmother, what great ears you have!"
"The better to hear you, my child!"

"Grandmother, what great eyes you have!"
"The better to see you, my child!"
"Grandmother, what great teeth you have!"
"The better to eat you!"

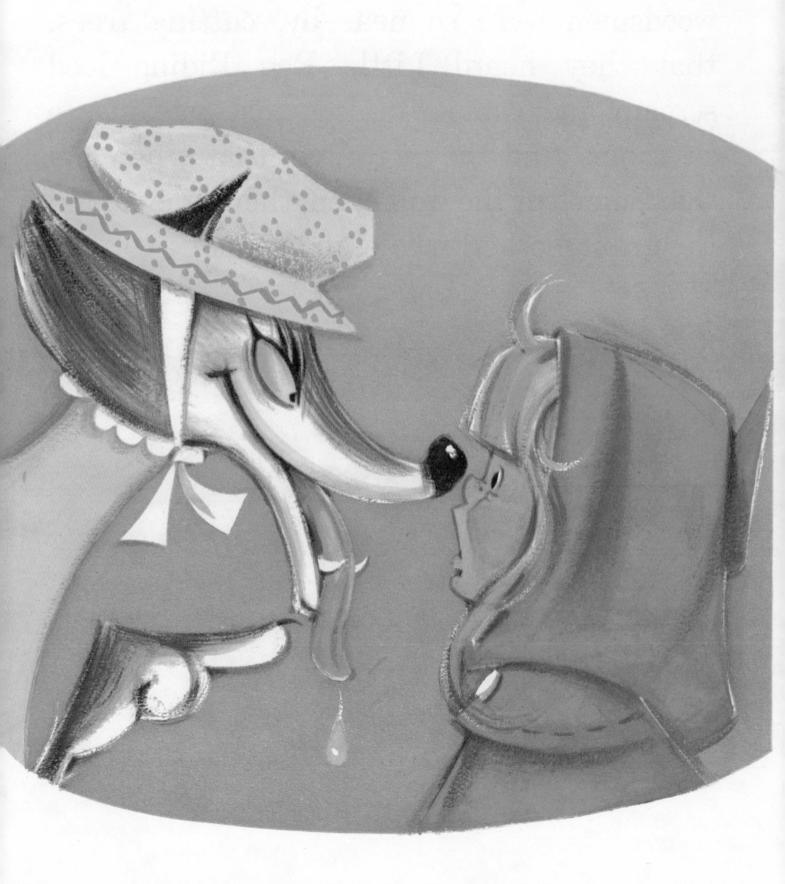

With these words the wicked wolf fell upon poor Little Red Riding-Hood.

And there the story ends. Nobody knows just what happened. Some say that the woodsmen were so near by, cutting trees, that they heard Little Red Riding-Hood scream and came running, just in time to save her. And they say, too, that when the woodsmen cut the wolf open, there they found the grandmother, whole and sound!

THE FOX AND THE GRAPES

A Fox one day spied a beautiful bunch of ripe grapes hanging from a vine trained along the branches of a tree. The grapes seemed ready to burst with juice, and the Fox's mouth watered as he gazed longingly at them.

The bunch hung from a high branch, and the Fox had to jump for it. The first time he jumped he missed it by a long way. So he walked off a short distance and took a running leap at it, only to fall short once more. Again and again he tried, but in vain.

Now he sat down and looked at the grapes in disgust.

"What a fool I am," he said. "Here I am wearing myself out to get a bunch of sour grapes that are not worth gaping for."

And off he walked very, very scornfully.

There are many who pretend to despise and belittle that which is beyond their reach.

THE BOYS AND THE FROGS

Some Boys were playing one day at the edge of a pond in which lived a family of Frogs. The Boys amused themselves by throwing stones into the pond so as to make them skip on top of the water.

The stones were flying thick and fast and the Boys were enjoying themselves very much; but the poor Frogs in the pond were trembling with fear.

At last one of the Frogs, the oldest and bravest, put his head out of the water, and said, "Oh, please, dear children, stop your cruel play! Though it may be fun for you, it means death to us!"

Always stop to think whether your fun may not be the cause of another's unhappiness.

THE ANTS AND THE GRASSHOPPER

One bright day in late autumn a family of Ants were bustling about in the warm sunshine, drying out the grain they had stored up during the summer, when a starving Grasshopper, his fiddle under his arm, came up and begged for a bite to eat.

"What!" cried the Ants in surprise, "haven't you stored anything away for the winter? What in the world were you doing all last summer?"

"I didn't have time to store up any food," whined the Grasshopper. "I was so busy making music that before I knew it the summer was gone."

The Ants shrugged their shoulders in disgust. "Making music, were you?" they cried. "Very well, now dance!" And they turned their backs on the Grasshopper and went on with their work.

There's a time for work and a time for play.

THE FOX AND THE GOAT

A Fox fell into a well, and though it was not very deep, he found that he could not get out again. After he had been in the well a long time, a thirsty Goat came by. The Goat thought the Fox had gone down to drink, and so he asked if the water was good.

"The finest in the whole country," said the crafty Fox. "Jump in and try it. There is more than enough for both of us."

The thirsty Goat immediately jumped in and began to drink. The Fox just as quickly jumped on the Goat's back and leaped from the tip of the Goat's horns out of the well.

The foolish Goat now saw what a plight he had got into, and begged the Fox to help him out. But the Fox was already on his way to the woods.

"If you had as much sense as you have beard, old fellow," he said as he ran, "you would have been more cautious about finding a way to get out again before you jumped in."

Look before you leap.

THE DOG AND HIS REFLECTION

A Dog, to whom the butcher had thrown a bone, was hurrying home with his prize as fast as he could go. As he crossed a narrow footbridge, he happened to look down and saw himself reflected in the quiet water as if in a mirror. But the greedy Dog thought he saw a real Dog carrying a bone much bigger than his own.

If he had stopped to think he would have
known better. But instead of thinking, he dropped
his bone and sprang at the Dog in the river, only
to find himself swimming for dear life to reach the
shore. At last he managed to scramble out, and as
he stood sadly thinking about the good bone he
had lost, he realized what a stupid Dog he had
been.

It is very foolish to be greedy.

THE SHEPHERD BOY AND THE WOLF

A Shepherd Boy tended his master's Sheep near a dark forest not far from the village. Soon he found life in the pasture very dull. All he could do to amuse himself was to talk to his dog or play on his shepherd's pipe.

One day as he sat watching the Sheep, and thinking what he would do should he see a Wolf, he thought of a plan to amuse himself.

His Master had told him to call for help should a Wolf attack the flock, and the Villagers would drive it away. So now, though he had not seen anything that even looked like a Wolf, he ran toward the village shouting, "Wolf! Wolf!"

As he expected, the Villagers who heard the cry dropped their work and ran in great excitement to the pasture. But when they got there they found the Boy doubled up with laughter at the trick he had played on them.

A few days later the Shepherd Boy again

shouted, "Wolf! Wolf!" Again the Villagers ran to help him, only to be laughed at again.

Then one evening as the sun was setting behind the forest, a Wolf really did spring from the underbrush and fall upon the Sheep.

In terror the Boy ran toward the village shouting, "Wolf! Wolf!" But though the Villagers heard the cry, they did not run to help him as they had before. "He cannot fool us again," they said.

The Wolf killed a great many of the Boy's sheep and then slipped away into the forest.

Liars are not believed even when they speak the truth.

THE CAT, THE COCK, AND THE YOUNG MOUSE

A very young Mouse, who had never seen anything of the world, almost came to grief the very first time he ventured out. And this is the story he told his mother about his adventures.

"I was strolling along very peaceably when, just as I turned the corner into the next yard, I saw two strange creatures. One of them had a very kind and gracious look, but the other was the most fearful monster you can imagine.

"On top of his head and in front of his neck hung pieces of raw red meat. He walked about restlessly, tearing up the ground with his toes, and beating his arms savagely against his sides. The moment he caught sight of me he opened his pointed mouth as if to swallow me, and then he let out a roar that frightened me to death."

Can you guess who it was that our young Mouse was trying to describe to his mother? It was nobody but the Barnyard Cock and the first one the little Mouse had ever seen.

"If it had not been for that terrible monster," the Mouse went on, "I should have made the acquaintance of the pretty creature, who looked so good and gentle. He had thick, velvety fur, a meek face, and his eyes were bright and shining. As he looked at me he waved his long tail and smiled.

"I am sure he was just about to speak to me when the monster I have told you about let out a screaming yell, and I ran for my life."

"My son," said the Mother Mouse, "that gentle creature you saw was none other than the Cat.

Under his kindly appearance, he bears a grudge against every one of us. The other was nothing but a bird who wouldn't harm you in the least. As for the Cat, he eats us. So be thankful, my child, that you escaped with your life, and, as long as you live, never judge people by their looks."

Do not trust alone to outward appearances.

THE WOLF IN SHEEP'S CLOTHING

A certain Wolf could not get enough to eat because of the watchfulness of the Shepherds. But one night he found a sheep skin that had been cast aside and forgotten. The next day, dressed in the skin, the Wolf strolled into the pasture with the Sheep. Soon a little Lamb was following him about and was quickly led away to slaughter.

That evening the Wolf entered the fold with the flock. But it happened that the Shepherd took a fancy for mutton broth that very evening, and, picking up a knife, went to the fold. There the first he laid hands on and killed was the Wolf.

The evil doer often comes to harm through his own deceit.

THE LION AND THE MOUSE

A Lion lay asleep in the forest, his great head resting on his paws. A timid little Mouse came upon him unexpectedly, and in her fright and haste to get away, ran across the Lion's nose. Roused from his nap, the Lion laid his huge paw angrily on the tiny creature to kill her.

"Spare me!" begged the poor Mouse. "Please

let me go and some day I will surely repay you."

The Lion was much amused to think that a Mouse could ever help him. But he was generous and finally let the Mouse go.

Some days later, while stalking his prey in the forest, the Lion was caught in the toils of a hunter's net. Unable to free himself, he filled the forest with his angry roaring. The Mouse knew the voice

and quickly found the Lion struggling in the net. Running to one of the great ropes that bound him, she gnawed it until it parted, and soon the Lion was free.

"You laughed when I said I would repay you," said the Mouse. "Now you see that even a Mouse can help a Lion."

A kindness is never wasted.

THE HARE AND THE TORTOISE

A Hare was making fun of the Tortoise one day for being so slow.

"Do you ever get anywhere?" he asked with a mocking laugh.

"Yes," replied the Tortoise, "and I get there sooner than you think. I'll run you a race and prove it."

The Hare was much amused at the idea of running a race with the Tortoise, but for the fun of the thing he agreed. So the Fox, who had consented to act as judge, marked the distance and started the runners off.

The Hare was soon far out of sight, and to make the Tortoise feel very deeply how ridiculous it was for him to try a race with a Hare, he lay down beside the course to take a nap until the Tortoise should catch up.

The Tortoise meanwhile kept going slowly but steadily, and, after a time, passed the place where the Hare was sleeping. But the Hare slept on very peacefully; and when at last he did wake up, the Tortoise was near the goal. The Hare now ran his swiftest, but he could not overtake the Tortoise in time.

The race is not always to the swift.

THE GOOSE AND THE GOLDEN EGG

There was once a Countryman who possessed the most wonderful Goose you can imagine, for every day when he visited the nest, the Goose had laid a beautiful, glittering, golden egg.

The Countryman took the eggs to market and soon began to get rich. But it was not long before he grew impatient with the Goose because she gave him only a single golden egg a day. He was not getting rich fast enough.

Then one day, after he had finished counting his money, the idea came to him that he could get all the golden eggs at once by killing the Goose and cutting it open. But when the deed was done, not a single golden egg did he find, and his precious Goose was dead.

Those who have plenty want more and so lose all they have.

THE NORTH WIND AND THE SUN

The North Wind and the Sun had a quarrel about which of them was the stronger. While they were disputing with much heat and bluster, a Traveler passed along the road wrapped in a cloak.

"Let us agree," said the Sun, "that he is the stronger who can strip that Traveler of his cloak."

"Very well," growled the North Wind, and at once sent a cold, howling blast against the Traveler.

With the first gust of wind the ends of the cloak whipped about the Traveler's body. But he immediately wrapped it closely around him, and the harder the Wind blew, the tighter he held it to him. The North Wind tore angrily at the cloak, but all his efforts were in vain.

Then the Sun began to shine. At first his beams were gentle, and in the pleasant warmth after the bitter cold of the North Wind, the Traveler unfastened his cloak and let it hang loosely from his shoulders. The Sun's rays grew warmer and warmer. The man took off his cap and mopped his brow. At last he became so heated that he pulled off his cloak, and, to escape the blazing sunshine, threw himself down in the welcome shade of a tree by the roadside.

Gentleness and kind persuasion win where force and bluster fail.

RIP VAN WINKLE

In a village near the Catskill
    Mountains,
Rip Van Winkle led a carefree life
In a tumble-down old house,
With his children and his wife.

On a bench beside the Village Inn,
Through a long summer's day,
Rip and his friends would sit
And talk the hours away.

Rip was a *special* friend
Of the village girls and boys.
He flew their kites and played their games
And mended all their toys.

"While you mend *toys*," cried his wife
    in a rage,
"The roof on our house is leaking!"
But Rip and his dog took to the woods
While his angry spouse was speaking.

As the mountains cast their shadows
And the sun sank low in the sky,
Rip beheld a man with a keg
Climbing the path nearby.

Rip hastened to offer assistance
And much to his surprise,
He found a dwarf-like fellow
With flowing beard and beady eyes.

Not a word had the stranger spoken
As they climbed to the mountaintop.
Sounds of thunder rumbled and rolled.
The little man motioned Rip to stop.

The peals of thunder grew closer,
Rumbling, rumbling, rolling.
Rip saw through the trees an open spot
Where more little men were bowling.

They were dressed like his companion.

There must have been eight or ten.

They stared at Rip in silence,

Then turned to their game again.

The ball made a noisy rumble
As it rolled along the ground.
Then it knocked the nine-pins down
With a crashing thunderous sound.

Rip grew weary of watching
This odd company at play.
He sat down to rest, but alas!
He fell sound asleep right away.

The birds were singing when Rip

woke up

And the sun was shining bright.

"What excuse shall I give my wife

For sleeping here all night?"

He didn't know that he was old,
With a beard that was long and white,
Or that he had slept for twenty years
Instead of just *one* night.

He whistled and called for his dog,
But Wolf was nowhere about.
All he could hear were the echoes
Returning his whistle and shout.

So Rip picked up his rusty gun
And hungry now for food,
He hobbled slowly home again
In a sad and troubled mood.

When he reached the village
People stopped to stare,
For Rip was a sight to behold
With his raggedy clothes and long
white hair.

"Does nobody know Rip Van Winkle?"
    he asked,
His eyes were filled with tears.
"Rip Van Winkle!" said two or three,
"Has been gone for twenty years!"

"It *is* Rip Van Winkle," said an old
    woman,
    As she tottered to his side.
"Where have you been these twenty
    years?
And here are your children," she cried.

On a bench beside the Village Inn,
As in the days long past,
Rip would tell his story
To strangers when they asked.

To this day when the village children
Hear the thunder rumbling . . . rolling,
They say that the little men
Are up in the mountains bowling.